Dolly Dolphin and
THE STRANGE NEW SOMETHING

A Sea World Book ™

© 1994 Sea World, Inc. All Rights Reserved

Sea World, the Whale Logo, and the Sea World Characters are trademarks of Sea World, Inc.
No part of this book may be reproduced or copied in any form or by any means —
graphics, electronic, or mechanical, including photo copying, taping, or information storage and
retrieval systems — without written permission of the publisher.

Published by

THIRD STORY BOOKS™
955 Connecticut Avenue, Suite 1302
Bridgeport, Connecticut 06607

ISBN 1-884506-07-0

Distributed to the trade by
Andrews & McMeel
4900 Main Street
Kansas City, Missouri 64112

Library of Congress Catalog Card Number: 93-61826

Printed in Singapore

Dolly Dolphin and
THE STRANGE NEW SOMETHING

A book about cooperation by DINA ANASTASIO

Illustrated by WILLIAM LANGLEY STUDIOS

THIRD™
STORY
BOOKS

Dear Grown-up:

When SEA WORLD opened its doors in 1964, it had a mission. That mission was to give adults and children a chance to see and learn about all the creatures of the sea . . . and to help preserve these creatures for future generations.

SEA WORLD books have a similar mission. They were created to entertain, and to help teach children something about the wonderful creatures that call the oceans home. And all books in this series are approved by the Education Department at SEA WORLD.

But SEA WORLD books teach kids other things, too—such as the importance of friendship, of self-esteem, of caring for our planet and for one another. Most importantly, SEA WORLD books accomplish their "missions" by telling stories about the wonderful creatures of the sea— stories your children will love to experience again and again.

By the way, when you've finished reading the story in this SEA WORLD book, don't forget to take a look at the two pages that follow the story. On them are some seaworthy facts about things in the story that you and your children might find interesting.

Welcome to SEA WORLD books. We hope your whole family enjoys them . . . and learns a little something from them, too!

Sincerely,
The Publishers

One morning, while Dolly Dolphin was playing alone in the clear sea, she heard a familiar sound. She rose up in the water and listened. Shamu was calling. He and Baby Shamu wanted to play.

Dolly shook her flippers and zoomed through the water. She was happy, because there was nothing that Dolly liked better than jumping and diving in the beautiful sea with her friends.

Dolly spent the rest of the morning playing in the waves with Shamu and Baby Shamu.

Suddenly, Dolly noticed a strange, new something moving through the water.

"Look, Shamu!" she said happily. "There's a new toy over there. Let's hurry and play with it."

And she flipped her tail into the air and was gone.

Now, Shamu had seen that strange, new something before. He had seen it wiggling, and floating, and twisting in oceans all over the world, and he did not like it at all.

He raised his head quickly and sang out to Dolly. It was a call filled with fear and alarm. "Stop, Dolly!" he cried. "Please, stop!"

Dolly heard Shamu and tried to turn back. But it was too late. The strange, new something was a net being pulled by a fishing boat — and it had accidentally caught her.

When Shamu saw what had happened, he knew what to do. *I've got to make that fishing boat stop!* he thought. *The people in it don't know that they've caught Dolly!*

Shamu swam to the front of the boat. With a huge sweep of his tail, he sent a giant wave of water up onto the deck.

"STOP THE BOAT!" shouted the people on board.

The boat had stopped. But, no one on the boat knew that Dolly was in their net.

"We have to let them know they've accidentally caught Dolly," said Baby Shamu. "But how?"

"I think it's time to get help," Shamu replied. Shamu opened his great mouth and called to his friends. His calls drifted through the air and echoed around the sea.

Nearby, in Codfish Cove, O.P. Otter heard Shamu's call.

"Listen, Clancy!" he said to his friend Clancy Clam. "It's Shamu!
Dolly's in trouble! Shamu needs us to help him. Quick! I'll ring the bell
to call the crew."

O.P. raced on board the FunShip. He rang the bell to alert everyone to the problem. Sir Winston Walrus and Virgil Pelican were the first to arrive.

"What's up?" asked Sir Winston.

"Dolly's in trouble!" O.P. replied. "She's been caught in a fishing net, and the fishermen don't know!"

"Then there's no time to lose," said Sir Winston. "Let's get under way!"

When everyone had gathered on the FunShip, Sir Winston set sail.

"If the fishermen knew that Dolly was in their net, they'd be sure to help her," said Sir Winston. "So our job is to try to tell them what the problem is."

The FunShip quickly skimmed across the water. Soon, O.P. Otter and Virgil Pelican spied the fishing boat and the net that was holding Dolly.

"Dolly on starboard, Sir Winston!" O.P. cried.

"Dolly on starboard," echoed Virgil.

"Now to alert the fishing boat!" said Sir Winston.

While the crew of the FunShip was busy figuring out what to do, Sydney the Shark was also on his way to the scene. He, too, had heard Shamu's calls.

Dolly's in danger, Sydney thought as he swam swiftly through the water. *I've got to get there in a hurry!*

Sydney the Shark soon reached the boat. He circled the fishing net. Around and around he went, moving his fin from side to side. The crew of the fishing boat immediately saw what was wrong.

"Look!" they shouted. "We've caught a dolphin! Quick! Let her go!"

The crew of the fishing boat opened the net and let Dolly out. Dolly jumped and squeaked happily, swimming in great circles.

"Great news!" Sir Winston called. "Dolly is fine!"

"I feel sorry for the crew of the fishing boat, though," said Penny Penguin. "When they let Dolly go, they lost all the fish they had caught."

Sir Winston thought for a moment.

"I think I know a way we can repay them," he said. He whispered something to Virgil Pelican. Virgil smiled and nodded. Then, with a flap of his wings, he lifted off the boat's railing and disappeared.

A few minutes later Virgil appeared above the fishing boat. He was ready.

Virgil opened his beak and leaned forward. One by one, the fish that he had gathered fell onto the fishing boat below.

"It's raining fish!" cried the people on the boat happily. "Now we won't have to go home with empty nets. Hurrah!"

"Thanks for all your help, Sir Winston!" called Shamu when Virgil had returned to the FunShip. "Your idea about the fish was great. Now the crew of the fishing boat won't go home empty-handed."

"You're welcome," Sir Winston replied. "Glad to be a part of the rescue team!"

That night Baby Shamu was almost too excited to sleep.

"We all helped save Dolly, didn't we, Shamu?" he asked.

"That's right," Shamu said. "We did it by working together. It took all of us — the FunShip, Sydney, you, me and the crew of the fishing boat, too — to get the job done."

"I'm glad that Dolly is all right," said Baby Shamu, beginning to doze off.

"So am I," Shamu agreed. "So am I."

Ahoy, There!

This is Shamu...and here
are some seaworthy facts for you!

Starboard

When the FunShip reaches Dolly, O.P. Otter calls, "Dolly on starboard!"
Do you know what *starboard* means?

Well, it doesn't mean there's an actor or actress on board Sir Winston's boat,
that's for sure! Starboard is a sailing term for *right*. O.P. was telling the others
that Dolly was on the starboard—or right—side of the boat.

Here are some other seaworthy words you might want to learn:

aft   the back of a boat ("Go aft!" means go to the back of the boat)

bow   the front part of a boat

galley   a boat's kitchen

head   a boat's bathroom

port   left (the opposite of starboard)

Fishy Fact

Did you know . . . that dolphins are really a kind of whale? And
that the horse is a cousin to the whale? Studies suggest that the
closest land-dwelling relatives of whales are mammals with hooves!

Port Out, Starboard Home *(posh)*

Do you know that the word posh — which means rich or expensive, or especially fancy — was originally a boating term? Well, it was!

Years ago, many people traveled from Great Britain to India by ship.

When you were leaving Great Britain to go to India, the best side of the ship to sit on was the port side. That's because the port side was shady . . . and the sun got very hot as you got closer to India.

But when you were coming home from India, it was the starboard side that was the shady one. So that was the best side to have your cabin on.

Port out, starboard home was the way that rich English people wanted to cruise to India and back. And the first letters of those four words—port out, starboard home—spell the word *posh!*

Fishing for Dolphins

Tuna and certain kinds of dolphins are often found together. So when people go fishing for tuna, sometimes dolphins get caught up in their nets.

People were afraid that if dolphins kept getting caught, they would soon become extinct. So in 1972 the U.S. Marine Mammal Protection Act was passed that made it illegal to hunt or harass any marine mammal in U.S. waters.

There are a few exceptions to this rule. Scientists and oceanaria like SEA WORLD can display these animals for research and humane purposes. This allows people to learn about these animals and about how we can help them to survive.

Sea World®

"For in the end we will conserve only what we love.
We will love only what we understand.
And we will understand only what we are taught."
Baba Dioum — noted Central African Naturalist

Since the first Sea World opened in 1964, more than 160 million people have experienced first-hand the majesty and mystery of marine life. Sea World parks have been leaders in building public understanding and appreciation for killer whales, dolphins, and a vast variety of other sea creatures.

Through its work in animal rescue and rehabilitation, breeding, animal care, research and education, Sea World demonstrates a strong commitment to the preservation of marine life and the environment.

Sea World provides all its animals with the highest-quality care including state-of-the-art facilities and stimulating positive reinforcement training programs. Each park employs full-time veterinarians, trainers, biologists and other animal care experts to provide 24-hour care. Through close relationships with these animals — relationships that are built on trust — Sea World's animal care experts are able to monitor their health every day to ensure their well-being. In short, all animals residing at Sea World are treated with respect, love and care.

If you would like more information about Sea World books, please write to us. We'd like to hear from you.

THIRD STORY BOOKS
955 Connecticut Avenue, Suite 1302
Bridgeport, CT 06607